P9-DOF-636

DISCARD

Sea Prayer

Sea Prayer

Khaled Hosseini

RIVERHEAD BOOKS

NEW YORK

2018

RIVERHEAD BOOKS
An imprint of Penguin Random House LLC
375 Hudson Street
New York, New York 10014

Copyright © 2017, 2018 by The Khaled Hosseini Foundation

This story, in a different version, formed the narration of
"Sea Prayer, a 360 story inspired by refugee Alan Kurdi," an
animated video published online by *The Guardian*.

Dan Williams's illustrations are published by arrangement
with Bloomsbury Publishing Plc. Copyright © 2018 by Dan
Williams.

Penguin supports copyright. Copyright fuels creativity,
encourages diverse voices, promotes free speech, and creates
a vibrant culture. Thank you for buying an authorized
edition of this book and for complying with copyright laws
by not reproducing, scanning, or distributing any part of it
in any form without permission. You are supporting writers
and allowing Penguin to continue to publish books for every
reader.

Library of Congress Cataloging-in-Publication Data

Names: Hosseini, Khaled, author.
Title: Sea prayer / Khaled Hosseini.
Description: New York : Riverhead Books, 2018.
Identifiers: LCCN 2018022980 (print) | LCCN 2018025919
(ebook) | ISBN 9780525539117 (e-book) | ISBN 9780525539094
(hardcover) | ISBN 9780525539100 (pbk.)
Subjects: LCSH: Syria—History—Civil War, 2011– —
Refugees—Fiction. | GSAFD: War stories
Classification: LCC PS3608.O832 (ebook) | LCC PS3608.O832
S44 2018 (print) | DDC 813/.6—dc23
LC record available at https://lccn.loc.gov/2018022980

Book design by Claire Vaccaro and Sandra Zellmer

Printed in the United States of America

10 9 8 7 6 5 4 3 2 1

R0453209712

This book is dedicated

to the thousands of refugees

who have perished at sea

fleeing war and persecution.

My dear Marwan,
in the long summers of childhood,
when I was a boy the age you are now,
your uncles and I
spread our mattress on the roof
of your grandfather's farmhouse
outside of Homs.

We woke in the mornings
to the stirring of olive trees in the breeze,
to the bleating of your grandmother's goat,
the clanking of her cooking pots,
the air cool and the sun
a pale rim of persimmon to the east.

We took you there when you were a toddler.

I have a sharply etched memory
of your mother from that trip,
showing you a herd of cows grazing in a field
blown through with wild flowers.

I wish you hadn't been so young.

You wouldn't have forgotten the farmhouse,

the soot of its stone walls,

the creek where your uncles and I built

a thousand boyhood dams.

I wish you remembered Homs as I do, Marwan.

In its bustling Old City,

a mosque for us Muslims,

a church for our Christian neighbors,

and a grand souk for us all

to haggle over gold pendants and

fresh produce and bridal dresses.

I wish you remembered
the crowded lanes smelling of fried kibbeh
and the evening walks we took
with your mother
around Clock Tower Square.

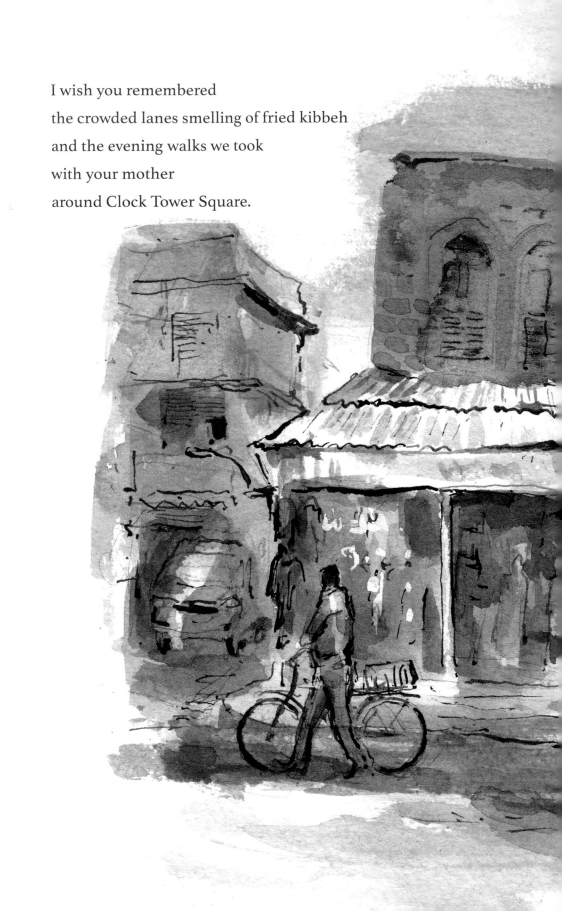

But that life, that time,
seems like a dream now,
even to me,
like some long-dissolved rumor.

First came the protests.

Then the siege.

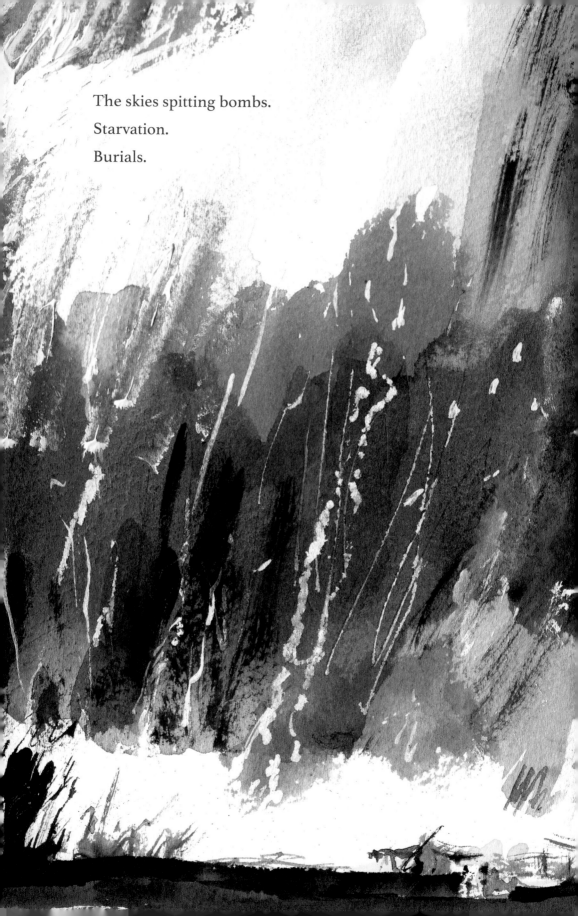

The skies spitting bombs.
Starvation.
Burials.

These are the things you know.

You know a bomb crater
can be made into a swimming hole.
You have learned
dark blood is better news
than bright.

You have learned that mothers and
sisters and classmates can be found
in narrow gaps between concrete,
bricks, and exposed beams,
little patches of sunlit skin
shining in the dark.

Your mother is here tonight, Marwan,
with us, on this cold and moonlit beach,
among the crying babies and
the women worrying
in tongues we don't speak.
Afghans and Somalis and Iraqis and
Eritreans and Syrians.
All of us impatient for sunrise,
all of us in dread of it.
All of us in search of home.

I have heard it said we are the uninvited.
We are the unwelcome.
We should take our misfortune elsewhere.

But I hear your mother's voice,

over the tide,

and she whispers in my ear,

"Oh, but if they saw, my darling.

Even half of what you have.

If only they saw.

They would say kinder things, surely."

I look at your profile
in the glow of this three-quarter moon,
my boy, your eyelashes like calligraphy,
closed in guileless sleep.

I said to you,
"Hold my hand.
Nothing bad will happen."

These are only words.

A father's tricks.

It slays your father,

your faith in him.

Because all I can think tonight is

how deep the sea,

and how vast, how indifferent.

How powerless I am to protect you from it.

All I can do is pray.

Pray God steers the vessel true,
when the shores slip out of eyeshot
and we are a flyspeck
in the heaving waters, pitching and tilting,
easily swallowed.

Because you,
you are precious cargo, Marwan,
the most precious there ever was.

I pray the sea knows this.
Inshallah.

How I pray the sea knows this.

Sea Prayer *was inspired by the story of Alan Kurdi, the three-year-old Syrian refugee who drowned in the Mediterranean Sea trying to reach safety in Europe in 2015.*

In the year after Alan's death, 4,176 others died or went missing attempting that same journey.